STALL BUDDIES

STALL BUDDIES

by **Penny Pollock**

illustrated by **Gail Owens**

G. P. Putnam's Sons
New York

Text copyright © 1984 by Penny Pollock
Illustrations copyright © 1984 by Gail Owens
All rights reserved. Published simultaneously in
Canada by General Publishing Co. Limited, Toronto.
Printed in the United States of America.
Book design by Virginia Evans

Library of Congress Cataloging in Publication Data
Pollock, Penny.
Stall buddies.
Summary: Scarlett, a nervous young filly from a fine
family of trotters, finds a home on a run-down farm in
Ohio, where she makes friends with a friendly rooster and
a motherless goat and calms down enough to fulfill her
promise as a harness racer.
1. Children's stories, American. [1. Horses—Fiction.
2. Harness racing—Fiction. 3. Domestic animals—Fiction]
I. Owens, Gail, ill. II. Title.
PZ7.P765St 1984 [Fic] 84-9947
ISBN 0-399-21118-7
First impression

For Bob Gilson . . . Wendy's stall buddy

This story took place in my imagination, but I like to think such friendships happen. One thing is certain, *Stall Buddies* could not have been written without the help of the folks at the Meadowlands Racetrack. The trainers, the drivers, the owners—even the trotters themselves—were helpful beyond my expectations. And in one of the barns beyond the track, I met real stall buddies. One of them was a fat goat that caused trouble. That's when this story began.

Special thanks go to Carol Hodes for reading the manuscript and to Bob Mulcahy, who opened the stable door for Scarlett, Rufus, and Merabel.

Contents

1
Fear Sweat

Scarlett yanked on her rope, but she could not escape. She was about to be sold at auction, just like the other one-year-old horses around her. Ever since dawn, strangers had examined Scarlett's eyes, her legs, her feet. She didn't care what the strangers thought of her. All she cared about was going home. Home to the sweet smell of fresh hay. Scarlett snorted, trying to blow away the smell that filled the auction barn. She'd never smelled that odor before, but she knew what it was—fear sweat.

One of the men who worked in the auction barn came into Scarlett's stall. She side-stepped away from him.

"Stand still," the groom barked and whacked her rump with the flat of his hand.

Scarlett was so nervous that her reddish

coat was wet with sweat. Her eyes widened with fear, revealing the whites of her eyeballs.

The groom looked cross and tired, but that wasn't Scarlett's fault. When he tried to run a metal comb through her forelock, she tossed her head. He grabbed hold of her forelock and roughly braided blue and red ribbons in her hair. Those were the colors of her home stable, and that is where she wanted to go. Home.

It was nearly time for the auction to start. People scurried around getting ready. Horses whinnied and snorted. Sparrows flitted through the rafters overhead, discussing what they saw.

Two of the sparrows landed above Scarlett's head and watched her in disgust. "It's the last time she'll wear her home colors," one said.

"They'll sell her for anything they can get," said the other. "Who wants a horse that can't stand still?"

Scarlett knew they were right about her being jumpy. Ever since she was born, the smallest noise, the smallest movement made her twitch. When she was taken from her mother and put into a stall by herself, she'd been so frightened she'd walked around and around, all day and all night.

The auction ring was on top of a hollow wooden platform. Scarlett's footsteps made spooky echoing sounds. It took two handlers to lead her to the center of the ring.

The ring was edged with yellow plastic things that looked like flowers but didn't smell like flowers. Scarlett snorted and tossed her head nervously.

When the auctioneer spoke into the microphone, his loud voice startled Scarlett. She laid back her ears. While the auctioneer described her fine parentage, Scarlett kept an eye on the people around the ring. Their paper programs rustled and fluttered in a disturbing way.

Two old men laughed at Scarlett's antics. "How'd you like to put a harness on that bundle of nerves?" one said.

"Anybody who hitches a sulky to her is asking for a wild ride," the other man agreed. "And it won't be across the finish line."

The bidding was slow. And the prices were

11

low. Too low for a filly from a fine family of trotters. Too low for a filly with a broad chest, a proud head and wide-set eyes. But it was just as the sparrows had said; no one wanted a horse, especially a trotter, that had "trouble" written on her sweat-stained coat.

"I have four hundred dollars," boomed the auctioneer. "Anybody give four fifty?"

"Four fifty," someone cried in a high screechy voice.

Scarlett whirled and whinnied.

"I have four fifty. Anybody give five?"

The huge auction hall was silent except for the noise of Scarlett's jittery prancing.

"Four fifty once. Four fifty twice," cried the auctioneer. "Four fifty . . ."

"Five hundred dollars," called a quiet voice from the far side of the ring.

Scarlett steadied long enough to look at the man who'd spoken. He was young and thin and shabby. His brown hair flopped over his forehead, nearly reaching his blue eyes. There was something about him that made Scarlett bring her ears forward.

"Sold!" cried the auctioneer.

One of the old men called across the ring.
"You'll regret that, Sonny."

2
A Bad Beginning

Scarlett's new owner, Bud Crammer, ignored the old man's warning and wrote out a check for the auctioneer. Bud's training farm was in Hiram, Ohio. Four Maple Farm, as it was called, resembled Bud. It was small, shabby, and full of dreams for better days.

Scarlett was shipped to Four Maple Farm the next day. The van was shadowy-dark and smelled of scared horses and musty August heat. She fought the van all the way from New Jersey, where she was born, to Ohio, where she was going to live whether she liked it or not. As the van roared along, she bucked and screamed and pulled on her tethering rope. When the van hit a pothole in the road, she yanked hard on the rope and it broke. She reared, hit the roof, and gashed her head. Blood ran across her forehead into her eyes.

And that's when she arrived at her new home.

The van stopped with a jolt. The rear door banged open and sunlight streamed inside, chasing the shadows. Scarlett swung her head around to see what was happening.

"Steady, steady." Scarlett cocked her ears as she recognized the man's voice.

Bud Crammer stood at her head, examining her cut. He looked upset. "Throw me a wet sponge, will you Smitty?" he called, but not too loudly.

Scarlett felt warm water run down her long nose and something soft clean the blood from her eyes. Bud talked soothingly as he worked and, although she didn't understand what he said, she understood what he wanted. He wanted her to trust him. She shivered. Could she?

Bud snapped a lead rope on her halter and with a gentle slap on her chest, backed her safely down the ramp, out of the van. But no sooner had her four feet touched the ground than a rag blew across the stable yard, coming straight at her. Scarlett reared.

15

"Steady, steady," Bud said, and Scarlett settled down. With her eyes wide, she let him lead her toward a wooden barn that needed paint. A collie raced from the barn barking and startled her.

The man named Smitty laughed. His wrinkled face matched his wrinkled overalls. "You sure did it this time," he said to Bud. "She's as high strung as a kite."

Scarlett nuzzled Smitty to find out how he smelled. Pipe smell. That wasn't so bad, but she didn't like his loud voice.

"I thought you were just going to the sale to look," Smitty said as they neared the barn. "Then you were meant to go to New York to do your shopping."

"That was my plan," Bud admitted. "But then I saw her. Take a good look at her. She's got the spirit to win."

"Sure," Smitty said with a laugh. "Just like all the others. Next you'll say our problems are nearly over. What did you use for money this time?"

Scarlett felt Bud stiffen. "Never mind."

Smitty slapped his thigh. "Don't tell me you

used the money you saved for Sally Wingfield's engagement ring?"

Bud was silent, and Scarlett knew he was worried.

A grey cat darted in front of her, heading for a drainpipe for a drink. Scarlett skittered sideways and almost stepped on the cat.

A rooster with a grand red and green and purple tail sat on the water barrel by the stable door. Scarlett eyed him uneasily.

"My, my," the rooster said. "Aren't we skittish."

Scarlett kicked her right hind foot in answer.

"Tut, tut," the rooster said and followed close at her heels, daring her to kick again.

Her new stall was in the corner of the barn. It was lighted by one cobwebby window. Scarlett balked, but Bud led her straight in and snapped the chain across the door.

Scarlett sniffed the sawdust covered floor and snorted. She was used to straw bedding.

Without waiting for an invitation, the rooster perched on the rim of the hayrack in the corner of the stall. "Bud can't afford straw," he said, as if he'd been asked.

As soon as Bud unsnapped the lead rope and left, Scarlett started to pace around the edge of her stall.

"Will you keep still," the rooster said in disgust. "You're enough to make me dizzy." He flapped his wings to catch his balance.

Scarlett ignored him and made another round of her stall.

"I'd call you a stall walker of the worst sort," the rooster went on, "and what we don't need around here is a horse who uses up her energy before she reaches the track."

Scarlett made another round.

"But Bud will know what to do if you don't settle down." The rooster snickered the way roosters do. "I am Rufus Jones the Third," he said, fluffing his feathers importantly. "I know all there is to know about Four Maple Farm, because I've got connections."

He waited for her to be impressed, but all she did was stand by the stall door, bobbing and weaving her head over the chain barrier.

Rufus went on anyway. "I know that Smitty, the groom, sneaks smokes in the oat room. I know Bud wants to marry Sally Wingfield, but he's making a mistake. She looks like a kitten, but she's a cat inside. And now that Bud spent the money for her diamond ring on you instead, she'll about scratch his eyes out and maybe yours, too."

With this last piece of information, Rufus flopped down and fluttered away looking pleased with himself.

It wasn't long before Bud came back to the stable with Sally Wingfield. She had soft grey eyes, but Scarlett saw the flecks of green hidden in the center.

Sally studied Scarlett. "So this is my competition," she said to Bud.

"Isn't she a beauty?" he asked, patting Scarlett's neck.

"I wouldn't go that far," Sally said and tapped the wall with her blood red nails. "Her legs are like straws and her knees are all bones. She's too scrawny to pull a stick behind her, let alone a sulky."

Bud laughed and brushed his hair from his eyes. "She's young, that's all. She's a winner, you'll see. By this time next year I'll be able to buy you the biggest diamond you ever saw."

Sally laughed in a meowing way and stalked off as if she'd heard enough.

The night was long and lonely. Creaking, sighing sounds crept through the barn. Was it only the wind? Scarlett paced and worried. At one point she thought she heard a horse in the next stall, but when she whinnied, no one whinnied back.

3
Caught in Crossties

Rufus Jones the Third returned with the dawn. After pecking a few dropped oats under Scarlett's feed bin, the rooster flapped to his perch on the hayrack and went right on talking as if he'd spent the night.

"I know Bud," he said. "He thinks he can train you to win big. When it comes to buying horses, he's got more dreams than a feed bag has oats."

"Are there other horses here?" Scarlett asked.

Rufus preened importantly. "First there was Tango," he began. "She ran into a rose bush and injured an eye. Then there was Roscoe. He couldn't win if he was the only horse on the track. He wasn't worth chicken feed, if you'll excuse the expression." Scarlett couldn't help a snicker of amusement.

Rufus cocked his head in a know-it-all way and continued, "Only Flint makes money now. But he is . . ."

"Flint?" Scarlett broke in. She wasn't sure she liked the sound of that name.

Rufus snickered. "Whispering Flint, I call him. He's in the next stall. He was in the pasture when you arrived, but he's anxious to meet you."

Scarlett walked to her stall door and leaned out over the chain. She looked to the right and there, staring her in the face with his ears flat, was a horse with the meanest eyes she'd ever seen. She leaped backward but not before Flint tried to rake her soft muzzle with his yellowed teeth.

"He bites," Rufus said.

"Thanks for warning me!" Scarlett paced around her stall faster than ever.

Restless days followed uneasy nights, and Scarlett did not settle down. Flint nudged a board loose between their stalls so he could whisper mean things to her. That made her edgier than ever. But, as the days passed, Scarlett grew used to the smell of sawdust on her floor and the chatter of Rufus Jones the Third. She was surprised to learn that the rooster knew as much about harness racing as he knew about Four Maple Farm.

"If Bud wants to stay in the business," Rufus said one morning, "he's going to have to train you early and train you hard."

Rufus was right. Scarlett's training started the next day.

After talking to her softly, Bud snapped a rope on either side of her halter. She didn't mind till he attached the ropes to rings on either side of her stall door.

As soon as Scarlett tried to move, the ropes jerked on the sides of her head. She felt trapped. She pulled backward but couldn't escape. She yanked and snorted and broke into a sweat.

"Steady now," Bud said, but Scarlett's eyes were rimmed with white and her ears were flat.

"Settle down, girl. Settle down," Bud said, but she couldn't settle down. Bud sighed and unsnapped the ropes.

He tried again the next day. And the next.

He kept his voice gentle and stroked her forehead. Finally she stood reasonably still between the crossties, and he slipped a sugar cube in her mouth.

As she crunched it, he patted her neck and smiled. Then he set her free, and she paced restlessly around her stall.

From then on she had to stand in the cross-ties almost every day. But when Bud tried to slip a bridle over her head, she was frightened all over again. Her skin rippled and her eyes showed white. Bud smoothed her mane with his fingers and took away the bridle.

But Scarlett still worried. What would happen next? She kept on walking her stall and bobbing her head. Then she went off her feed.

Bud and Smitty watched her pace round and round, passing her full feed bin. Finally Bud said something to Smitty and walked away. Scarlett didn't know what Bud had said, but Rufus understood everything. As soon as they were alone, he crowed, "I knew they'd get you a stall buddy."

Scarlett quivered. "What's a stall buddy?"

"You'll see," Rufus said and plopped down from the hayrack and swaggered away.

4
Uninvited Company

At night, when Scarlett was alone with her worries, she paced more than ever. But during the day she was too busy to worry about anything, because Bud was pushing her training.

Gradually she grew used to the smell of leather, and after a good deal of coaxing, she let him slip the bridle over her head. Eventually she accepted the bit in her mouth, but not till Bud had warmed the metal with his hands. A few weeks later she felt the snugness of the girth against her belly.

Although her training was going well, she was still jumpy. When the collie barked, she shied. When the cat ran beneath her feet, she side-stepped. And when she was in her stall, she paced and stayed off her feed.

At the end of the week, Bud let her loose in

the pasture. She ran till her knees ached and her lungs burned, but she loved it. Smitty and Bud watched her and were smiling when they brought her back to the barn.

Rufus was waiting on the water barrel. "You've got company," he said as Scarlett pranced by.

She tossed her head and snorted. "Who is it?"

"See for yourself," Rufus said.

A small white thing was curled up in the middle of the sawdust on the stall floor. Scarlett snorted and balked, but Bud laughed and made her go in. He unsnapped her lead rope and fastened the chain across her door and left. Scarlett was alone with her visitor.

She walked closer and leaned down to sniff. Her visitor smelled alive but didn't move. Curious, and a little frightened, Scarlett lipped the white lump to see what would happen.

The white lump sprang to its skinny legs and bawled, "I want my mother!"

Scarlett jumped back and bumped her rump on the feed bin.

"I want my mother!" the white thing wailed again and drooped its head between its front legs.

Scarlett whinnied softly. The white thing blundered toward her, its legs all wobbly. As Scarlett watched, the smells and warmth of her own mother came back to her. Her mother's body had been warm, her milk sweet. Scarlett remembered the terrible night she was taken from her mother.

She took a step toward her teetering guest and nudged it with her nose to see if it bit or kicked. The white thing fell to the floor and struggled back on its trembling legs. "Are you my new mother?" it asked, sniffing up at Scarlett's belly.

"No," Scarlett said, "but . . . but I'm your friend."

The ball of white fluff hid under Scarlett and stretched up to rub her budding horn on Scarlett's side. "I'm Merabel," she said.

"And I'm . . ." Scarlett began, but before she could finish, Rufus swaggered into the stall.

"Ain't love grand," he said and fluttered up to his perch.

"Don't mind him," Scarlett said. "He's just Rufus."

"Rufus Jones the Third," the rooster corrected. "And you, Merabel, are one scrawny goat."

Scarlett pushed the rooster with her nose. "Mind your own business for once."

"Tut tut," Rufus said. "Aren't we the motherly one." He plopped to the floor and strutted away with his grand purple, red, and green tail gleaming in the twilight.

That night, after Smitty brought a bucket of milk for Merabel and sweet grain for Scarlett, the baby goat settled down to sleep. Scarlett hovered over her and tried not to move too much. She didn't want to step on someone soft and warm who missed her mother.

5
Crunch

When the weather became frosty, the pink hollyhock by the water barrel dropped its petals. The grass in the pasture turned yellow and the maple trees turned red.

Scarlett was taken to the training track for the first time. The track was on the far side of the barn. It was made of packed dirt with a ribbon of faded grass running between the lanes.

Smitty held her head while Bud tied short lengths of clothesline to either side of her bridle. Scarlett swung her head from side to side to see what was going on.

"Steady, steady," Bud said and pulled gently on one of the ropes so she'd get used to the feel of it.

She swung around so fast that Smitty was flung to the ground. Bud lunged to grab

Scarlett's bridle when she tried to rear.

"She needs time to get used to the short lines," Bud said and led her back to the barn.

"Wait till we try the long lines!" Smitty said, dusting off the seat of his pants.

The next day did not go any better. Smitty swore she wasn't worth the tobacco in his pipe.

It took a good many weeks, but Scarlett finally accepted the short lines and the long lines, too. The long lines were so long that Bud stood way behind her and held the ropes in his hands. When he pulled on the right-hand rope, she turned right. When he pulled the left-hand rope, she turned left.

Meanwhile, Merabel's belly grew fat and her nubby horns grew long enough to use for scratching. When Scarlett returned from the track feeling tense from all she had to learn, Merabel would scratch her flank until she relaxed. Then they'd both enjoy a good feed. Now that Merabel was eating grain, Scarlett ate it, too. She had to set a good example for her little friend. They shared their grain and water by day and slept head to tail at night.

At first, the only time they were apart was when Scarlett left for training. Merabel did not like being left behind so she bleated the whole time Scarlett was gone. Then Merabel started leaving the stall herself, just to tease. She'd hide behind harness bags or bales of hay. Sometimes she hid in the empty stalls. Scarlett did not think Merabel's game was funny. The minute the goat was out of sight, Scarlett started to worry. She'd call and call, but Merabel came back when she was ready and not a minute before.

Flint complained of all the noise, but Rufus crowed with self-satisfaction. "I knew you'd be good stall buddies," he said one morning. Then he announced it was time to start his racing instructions. "Now, when you're harnessed to the training cart for the first time, you have to remember that . . ."

Scarlett was not listening. She was pacing around, calling Merabel. The goat had wandered out of the stall hours ago. "Rufus," Scarlett said, "stop your chatter and go find Merabel."

Rufus preened his fine tail. "She's just teas-

34

ing," he said. "You're worse than a mother, worrying all the time."

"Rufus Jones the Third," Scarlett said and swatted him off his perch with one swish of her tail. "Go find Merabel."

"Okay, okay, take it easy," he said and waddled off.

When he didn't come back right away, Scarlett grew frantic. Something must have happened to the goat. She never stayed away this long. Scarlett tried to bite through the metal chain barrier. Then she struck at it with her hind feet. All the while she whinnied with worry.

Smitty came running. Scarlett was in a lather and the fear showed in her eyes. He tried to calm her, but couldn't, and then Rufus began squawking at the top of his lungs.

"What next?" Smitty said and raced off to find the rooster.

Rufus was circling a very sick goat. Merabel had hidden in the oat room and helped herself to an open sack of grain. Actually, she stuffed herself. She ate so much and so fast that she accidently swallowed Smitty's hidden tobacco pouch, metal clasp and all.

Rufus flapped back to Scarlett with the news. That night the little goat lay still as death, and Scarlett licked and lipped and nuzzled her till daybreak.

But Merabel was back to her tricks in a few days. Not only did she tease Scarlett, she began to boss her, too. If Scarlett bobbed her head, Merabel butted her flank. If Scarlett paced, Merabel blocked her way. If Scarlett went off her feed, Merabel wouldn't eat either.

The days that Flint went out to race were more peaceful than other days, even though he seldom won. But then one day he brought in a thousand-dollar win and whispered between the boards, "Someone's got to pay the bills."

"From what I hear," Rufus cried, "it was nag's day at the fair."

Flint showed his yellow teeth.

Merabel hated to miss anything, and since she couldn't see Flint from inside the stall, she went out for a look.

"Don't go near him!" Scarlett cried.

But Merabel was already going into Flint's stall. A second later there was a terrible crunching sound as he nipped off her left horn. Her howl of pain shook the boards of the old barn.

6
Jitters

Deep snow put an end to training. The barn was steamy hot with horse warmth. Flint shifted moodily in his stall. The nub of Merabel's horn healed, but it was never again as long as the other one. Scarlett said she liked her friend's lopsided appearance. Rufus said it didn't matter if Merabel had one horn or six, it was time for Scarlett to listen to him lecture on racing.

His instructions went on half the night, so he started to sleep in the hayrack. Scarlett listened and worried. What if she didn't win?

"Stay close to the rail like I tell you," Rufus said. "And try for second position so the lead horse cuts the wind for you, but don't get boxed in. Don't get parked out, either."

"Boxed in? Parked out?" Scarlett started to pace her stall.

Rufus sighed. "Don't you know anything

about harness racing? I mean don't let anyone block your way and don't get stuck on the outside of the track."

It was Scarlett's turn to sigh. If only Rufus could race for her.

"Now remember to save energy for the home stretch . . ." The lessons were endless.

Scarlett bobbed her head and listened. The weeks passed slowly. Smitty complained of all the work, and Bud complained of all the bills. Sally Wingfield came by twice, but each time she and Bud quarreled and she left in a huff.

At last the smell of spring mud filled the barn. The vet came to check Scarlett. The blacksmith came to fit her shoes. Smitty trimmed and shaved her forelock and mane. One day he braided her forelock with green and white ribbons, the colors of Four Maple Farm. Once she accepted all the fuss, he unbraided the ribbons and set her free.

"Bud's getting you used to being fancied up for your first race," Rufus said. "I think he's rushing things. You've just gotten used to the weight of the harness, and you've only pulled the jog cart twice."

39

Merabel pressed close to Scarlett's side. "She's ready to win any race she wants," Merabel said and jutted out her stubborn chin.

Scarlett trained hard and tried not to worry about the cart that was always behind her. But she'd never forget the first day the shafts of the jog cart were slipped through her harness straps. She'd tried to outrun the cart. Bud had leaped on the cart and pulled hard on the reins. Scarlett had fought the reins and the cart till she learned that the faster she trotted, the faster the cart went.

She still didn't like the tug of the cart, but it was attached to her harness every day. And every day she was taken to the training track

for exercise. Through wind and rain and
blistering heat, Bud handled the reins. On
certain days Bud urged her to trot as fast as
she could, while Smitty kept an eye on his
stopwatch.

"Four minutes," he called one day as
Scarlett trotted past him. She could feel Bud's
worry through the reins.

The next day she put out more power, and
Smitty gave her extra grain. A week later she
pulled a sulky for the first time. It was lighter
than the jog cart, and she improved her time.

Flint took a second at Moravia Downs in New York State. The barn could hardly hold his boasting.

"That won't pay the vet," Rufus said and returned to Scarlett's lessons. "Whatever you do, don't break stride. Trot as fast as you can, but don't gallop. If you do, you'll be taken to the outside of the track and lose your place."

Everyone had the jitters the night before Scarlett's first race. Bud quarreled with Sally worse than ever. Smitty smoked. Flint was silent. Merabel ate too much. Rufus went hoarse with last-minute reminders, and Scarlett went off her feed.

It was a sparkling day in June, and the stands were packed. The air crackled with noise from the loudspeaker and the rustle of a hundred programs. Flags snapped in the breeze. Scarlett fought the scared feeling that swelled inside her.

Bud wore the green and white colors that matched the ribbons in Scarlett's hair. Bud was excited as he mounted the sulky. Scarlett was scared.

The starting gate was attached to the back bumper of a car. Scarlett thought it was strange looking. She shied when Bud tried to line her up next to the other horses behind the gate.

"Steady now," Bud said. Scarlett tried to listen to his calm voice, but all she heard was the thudding of her own heart.

A tremendous roar broke from the grandstands as the car that carried the starting gate sped off and the race began. Scarlett started off in third place. Bud talked to her through the reins, but she couldn't pull ahead. Bud shifted his weight and gently slapped the reins.

Scarlett's pounding hooves scuffed up swirls of dust that filled her nostrils. All around her horses sweated and snorted and strained. Scarlett moved to second place and grabbed the rail. The crowd cheered, and Scarlett wished Merabel and Rufus could see her. Thinking of them, she trotted faster.

On the far turn she smelled the home stretch and opened up. Bud had to hold her from a gallop. She pulled out to pass the lead

horse. Thirty yards from the finish line, a red balloon blew down across the track. She saw it from the corner of her eye, coming straight for her feet. She bolted sideways and three horses swept by her.

The barn was quiet that night. Scarlett stood with her head hidden in the corner. Rufus tucked and retucked his feathers, and Merabel's soft bleatings were like a sad song.

45

7

A Splintering Crash

The next day it was Flint's turn to race. Bud and Smitty fussed over him and ignored Scarlett. She felt worse than ever.

Flint brought in a first. Scarlett, Merabel, and Rufus were forced to hear all the details. Flint whispered through the boards that Bud was relieved to have one horse who could win.

The following day rain drummed on the roof in a dreary beat. Sally Wingfield came to visit. Her grey raincoat matched her grey scarf and her grey kitten eyes. Scarlett saw the spark of green still hidden there. Rufus was right—Sally was pure cat underneath.

"So this was your sure winner," Sally said to Bud.

He fidgeted unhappily. "It was only her first race, and I pushed her too hard."

Sally sort of meowed that Bud always had an excuse for losing.

"Maybe you ought to keep your opinions to things you understand," he said and kicked an empty feed bag out of the way.

"There's one thing I understand perfectly well," Sally cried. "All you care about are your smelly horses and . . ."

"And all you care about is yourself!" Bud broke in.

Sally's grey eyes rippled with green. Her claws flexed. She and Bud yelled terrible things all the way out of the barn.

"I like her," Flint whispered.

"You would," Rufus said and turned his attention to Scarlett. "What you need is a shadow roll. Then you won't see the ground near you and you won't be scared by stuff on the track."

Rufus was right as usual. When Bud put a shadow roll around her head, below her eyes, Scarlett stopped worrying about objects on the ground. The next week she came in second at a county fair. The following week she took a first at Moravia Downs with a time of 2:05. That night the three friends celebrated their first win. Rufus crowed. Merabel bleated, and Scarlett pranced with pleasure.

Flint sulked.

When he raced the next day, Flint still felt sour and snappish. He came back to the barn feeling worse because on the second turn he'd crowded another horse, and the horse had crowded back. The wheels of their sulkies had locked. Flint had reared to free himself, and Bud had fallen off. He'd been carried from the track with his leg broken just above the ankle.

The barn was so quiet that night that not even the wind dared stir. Merabel slept curled under Scarlett, and Rufus roosted on top of the filly's back.

The next morning, Rufus said, "We can't waste time like this. We have to race in two days."

"But how can we race without Bud?" Scarlett asked, weaving her head nervously.

"Bud will have to hire a catch driver."

"What's a catch driver?" Merabel asked.

"Almost any driver Bud can hire. The trouble with catch drivers is that they don't have time to get to know the horse they're driving."

"That sounds scary," Merabel said and

rubbed her horn on Scarlett's flank.

Scarlett started to pace, and this time her friends let her.

The catch driver had a bristly mustache, and he smelled like moldy grain. Scarlett understood he was the only driver Bud could find. She was edgy as they lined up at the starting gate. She threw her head and side-stepped.

"Stop your fussing!" the driver yelled and snapped the reins hard across her sweaty back.

Scarlett's skin rippled with fear, but she promised herself she'd win this race. She'd win it for Rufus and Merabel and Bud.

She started off on the outside, but she wasn't worried. There was time to move in after the half-mile pole. Her driver thought differently. He slashed her with his whip and bellowed for her to step out.

Scarlett had never felt the sting of a whip. She slowed down, wondering what it was. It stung her wet back again and she went wild with fear.

She leaped sideways and broke into a gal-

lop. She jumped the inside rail, dragging the sulky behind her. The cart tilted and went over sideways with a splintering crash. The driver landed on his head and yowled with pain. Scarlett bucked and reared in terror.

No one could catch her head till she heard the quiet, "Steady, steady," of Bud's voice. He'd been watching the race from the side of the track. As soon as he saw she was in trouble, he'd hobbled across the track, crutches and all. He held her steady and patted her lathered neck. She looked at his face and saw that the dream of winning had left his eyes. She hung her head in shame.

8
Final Instructions

Smitty brought Scarlett sweet grain that night, but she wasn't tempted. She felt too miserable to eat, and not even her friends could cheer her up. Rufus kept saying it was all the driver's fault, and Merabel agreed. But Scarlett knew differently. She'd angered the man by misbehaving at the starting gate. Would she ever learn?

Smitty took over the training till Bud was off the crutches. Scarlett tried to trot faster than ever, but her feet felt as heavy as her heart. She was not raced all week, and she knew it was just as well.

A week later she felt worse. "We're finished for sure," Rufus grumbled. "You'll probably both be sold and I'll lose my cushy job."

"What's happened?" Scarlett asked.

"Bud's just found out that the sulky can't be fixed."

"Can't he rent one?" Merabel asked.

"What would he use for money?" Rufus said and flopped away with his feathers all bedraggled.

Three days later Rufus looked perky again. Bud had sold his car and used the money to rent a sulky. When the sulky was delivered, hope came back to Bud's eyes, and the friends were excited again. Rufus scurried out for more news and reported that evening.

"I think Bud's lost his mind," he began. "He's going to bet everything he owns on winning at the Meadowlands Racetrack in New Jersey."

"Is that an important track?" Merabel asked.

"Only one of the top tracks in the country," Rufus said, some of his old puffiness coming back.

"When are we going?" Scarlett asked.

"The first week of August."

Scarlett started to walk around her stall. August was only four weeks away. She'd never be ready.

Jogging, training, grooming filled every day. In the morning, Flint was worked out first. Then it was Scarlett's turn. Bud drove the jog cart with his leg still in a cast. Scarlett felt the extra weight and stepped out faster to make up for it. When she won a race with a time of 2:03, the dream began to grow in Bud's eyes. Rufus concentrated on the big race in New Jersey and lectured more than ever.

"There will be a week of racing, you know," he said.

"All week?" Merabel bleated.

Rufus nodded importantly. "Scarlett will race some days, and Flint will race the others."

"I'll win the big race," Flint whispered between the boards.

For once they hoped he was right.

August came and it was time to load into the double van, heading for New Jersey. Scarlett had been born in New Jersey, but she didn't think of it as home anymore. Now she belonged with Merabel and Rufus at Four Maple Farm.

Flint was loaded first, then Scarlett. Merabel cried till Bud gave in and let her scuttle in next to Scarlett.

Rufus had said his goodbyes and given his final instructions the night before. He was nowhere in sight when the van's door was bolted shut.

Scarlett and Merabel huddled close as the van rumbled away from Four Maple Farm. They'd only gone a mile when something red and green and purple fluttered up from beneath the straw at their feet.

"Rufus!" Scarlett cried. "How did you get here?"

"I've got connections," he said. "Now listen to me. We've got work to do." The lessons began all over again, and Scarlett and Merabel—and Flint—listened all the way from Ohio to the gates at the Meadowlands Racetrack.

The huge stables were alive with bustle and excitement. Racing colors of every shade of red and yellow, green and violet, flapped in the breeze. Harness was being lathered. Hay was being stacked. Horses were being walked to cool down and others were being harnessed for exercise. Everyone was nervous. Everyone wanted to win.

The week started off poorly for Scarlett. She was too jumpy to race well. She took a tenth and a sixth. Bud turned quiet. Smitty smoked. Flint whispered. Merabel prayed.

A young woman named Nina offered to help Bud. Her hair was like plaited straw, and she smelled of sweet grain. Bud smiled back at her and said he needed all the help he could get.

"She's the one for Bud," Merabel said.

Rufus shook his head in disgust. "As glad as I am to see the last of Sally Wingfield," he said, "this is no time for romance. We all have to help Flint win the next race."

"Don't worry," Flint whispered back. "Nobody stops Flint."

But someone did. A bay with four white hooves and eyes meaner than mean stopped Flint with one swift kick in his chest. Flint had crossed the wrong horse. The gash was jagged and ran deep. Flint wouldn't race again for a long time. Smitty nearly chewed the end off his pipe, and Bud's eyes looked hollow.

"Now it's all up to you," Rufus told Scarlett.

She shivered and hid her head in the corner.

9
A Timely Jab

The day before the big race, Scarlett was so tense she couldn't eat, and Merabel was so worried she couldn't stop eating. And then Rufus slunk into the stall with the worst news of all. A man with sneaky eyes and a hard mouth had watched Scarlett every time she raced. If she lost the big race, Bud was going to have to sell her, and this man was going to buy her.

"Why doesn't Bud sell Flint instead?" Merabel asked.

"Who'd want him?" Rufus said.

Flint shifted unhappily in the next stall.

Merabel rubbed Scarlett's flank with her horn. "Even if Bud has to sell us, we'll all stay together."

"No we won't!" Rufus cried. "This man doesn't believe in stall buddies. Besides that, he says roosters make him nervous and goats smell like cheese."

None of them slept that night. Scarlett looked inside herself for hope but didn't find any. Rufus tucked and retucked his feathers. Merabel complained that her stomach hurt.

At midnight Merabel slipped under the chain across the stall door and left. Dawn came, but she hadn't returned. Scarlett whinnied. Rufus searched. No Merabel.

Bud and Smitty came in the morning, but they were too weary with worry to notice that the goat was gone. Scarlett was frantic and fought being harnessed to the jog cart. All she wanted to do was to go find Merabel.

At last Smitty and Bud had her ready and on the track for her first warm-up lap before the race. Scarlett trotted slowly around the track, going in the opposite direction of the actual race. As she went along, her muscles loosened, but her fear tightened. What had happened to her friend?

When the warm-up ended, Bud's friend Nina was waiting by the barn. She helped sponge Scarlett with horse shampoo and then wiped off the water with an aluminum scraper. Smitty threw a light mesh blanket over Scarlett's back and walked her till she cooled off. Normally, Scarlett loved all this fuss, but today she shivered with impatience. She wanted to talk to Rufus. He must have found Merabel by now.

But when she saw Rufus drooped over the wheel of an empty sulky, she knew the news wasn't good. "Have you looked for her in the tack room?" Scarlett asked as Smitty walked her along.

"I've tried every room in the stable," Rufus said. "You better forget Merabel for now and think about winning this race."

They both knew this wasn't possible.

The second warm-up came, and there still was no sign of Merabel. But at post time, just before the big race, Merabel was carried to the stall on a board. She'd eaten six quarts of

oats, half a bale of alfalfa, and three bars of leather soap before collapsing under a van.

It took all of Smitty's and Bud's and Nina's strength to harness Scarlett to the sulky. She did not want to race. She wanted to take care of Merabel. It took so long to get Scarlett ready that they were late for the post parade and almost lost their position at the starting gate.

"Steady now, you can do it," Bud called to her.

Scarlett's skin rippled with tension. If she lost the race, she'd be sold and separated from her friends. But if Merabel died, what difference would it make? Nothing would matter then.

Scarlett got off to a slow start because she kept turning her head toward the stables. Two greys and a bay boxed her in before she knew it. Bud talked to her through the reins and she tried to listen. But she couldn't find the spirit to move out.

They passed the quarter pole. One of the greys pulled ahead and left an opening. Scarlett moved to the outside. Then the grey slowed a bit, and Scarlett was by his side. Her mind was half on the race and half on Merabel. Without thinking, Scarlett moved too near the grey, and the wheels of their sulkies locked. Scarlett panicked and tried to pull away. Bud worked the reins like an expert and with a screeching sound, the wheels broke free. The grey lunged ahead. Scarlett fell farther behind.

Her only chance was getting to the rail. She tried to move in, but the way was blocked. She was stuck on the outside of the track. She could feel Bud's worry through the reins as they passed the half-mile pole and she still lagged behind in third place. Scarlett tried to trot faster, but her knees ached, her lungs burned, and all she could think of was Merabel lying—perhaps dying—in the barn.

When she smelled the home stretch, Scarlett tried to open up. She gained on the grey in front of her, but she could not pass him. Her shadow roll kept her from seeing the red and green and purple fluster of feathers flap across the track and leap on her sulky. But she knew something was happening when Bud jerked the reins and cried out in surprise. Scarlett nearly lost her position trying to see what was going on.

Then she heard Rufus squawk at the top of his lungs, "Merabel's fine. NOW MOVE IT!"

Scarlett moved to the side of the grey but made sure their sulkies didn't touch. The crowd roared. Scarlett lifted her head and pointed her ears forward. Merabel was fine! Merabel was fine!

Inch by inch she gained on the grey and was nearly up to the lead horse, the bay. But then a swift chestnut came from behind and raced by her side. Scarlett fought for the second position, but the chestnut pulled ahead.

Scarlett was back in third place, and the finish line was in sight. Rufus, still clinging to the sulky for dear life, gave Scarlett's rump a vicious peck. "Pull out or you'll feel a lot worse," he crowed.

Scarlett surged ahead, ignoring her knees, forgetting her burning chest. Bud gave her her head, and Scarlett swept by the chestnut and trotted neck and neck with the bay. He was a fine gelding with eyes full of winning.

Rufus gave her rear another no-nonsense jab, and Scarlett leaped forward to win by a nose. The stands exploded with cheers. Flags snapped. Balloons flew. Programs fluttered.

Smitty tossed his pipe in the air in excitement and laughed when the ashes fell on his head. Nina ran up with Merabel in a wheelbarrow, and even above Nina's cheers, Scarlett could hear Merabel's happy bleating. Rufus flapped around in a tizzy, and Bud grabbed Nina's hands to dance.

Commotion swirled all around Scarlett, but she stood perfectly still—in the winner's circle.